Jeremy, Barnabas, and the Wonderful Dream

to Steve Estes,
my favorite storyteller

Chariot Books is an imprint of David C. Cook Publishing Co.
David C. Cook Publishing Co., Elgin, Illinois 60120
David C. Cook Publishing Co., Weston, Ontario

JEREMY, BARNABAS, AND THE WONDERFUL DREAM

Design by Catherine Colten

First printing, 1987
Printed in the United States of America
97 96 95 94   8 7 6 5

Library of Congress Cataloging-in-Publication Data
Tada, Joni Eareckson.
    Jeremy, Barnabas, and the wonderful dream / by Joni Eareckson Tada; illustrated by Ann Neilsen.
        p. cm.
    Summary: Jeremy's well-intentioned efforts to help with the chores on his uncle's farm wreak havoc, but a nocturnal conversation with Barnabas the cat convinces him that God makes all things work together for good.
    ISBN 1-555-13802-0
    [1. Farm life—Fiction. 2. Cats—Fiction. 3. Christian life—Fiction.] I. Neilsen, Ann, ill. II. Title.
PZ7.T116Je 1987
[E]—dc19   87-18338
                                                                                CIP
                                                                                AC

Jeremy threw back the big quilt. Was it the chickadees chitchatting on the windowsill that woke him? Or was it the delicious smell of Aunt Jeannie's pancakes and sausage? Or was it just plain old excitement? This was the first morning of his vacation on Uncle Dave's farm!

As he pulled on his jeans and boots, Jeremy planned his day. He couldn't wait to explore the farmhouse with its long staircase, high ceilings, and many nooks and crannies; build a fort in the barn loft with bales of straw; and—most important—help Uncle Dave with the chores. As he threw the quilt back over the bed, he prayed that he would do a good job. He knew Uncle Dave was counting on him.

Jeremy stamped down the stairs and jumped the last two steps to the floor, startling Barnabas, the friendly orange farm cat. Barnabas had been staring at the swinging pendulum in the grandfather clock, but now he turned to follow Jeremy to the kitchen. Together they ate breakfast, Jeremy enjoying a double helping of pancakes while Barnabas lapped fresh cream from his bowl.

Although he wanted to catch up with Uncle Dave down at the barn, Jeremy didn't rush through his breakfast. He leaned on his elbow and watched Aunt Jeannie. While she sipped her coffee, she read the Bible by her plate.

"God causes all things to work together for good to those who love Him," Aunt Jeannie read aloud.

Jeremy smiled and felt all cozy inside. Then the clock in the hallway chimed.

"I'm leaving to milk the cows now," Jeremy said. He carried his dishes to the sink and ran outside. Barnabas slipped through the screen door before it slammed and followed Jeremy to the barn.

Uncle Dave was at the pasture gate already, calling the cows in from the meadow. He waved when he saw Jeremy.

"You can start by scooping a bucket of grain into each stall. Do you remember how to unlatch the feed-bin door?" Uncle Dave pulled the gate open farther for old Bessie and the rest of the herd.

Jeremy gave Uncle Dave the thumbs-up sign and darted for the barn.

This is easy, thought Jeremy, as he hurriedly scooped buckets of grain and ran to each stall. He wanted to finish quickly to impress Uncle Dave. He knew he could do a lot more than his uncle realized. Within minutes, he raced back to the pasture gate.

Uncle Dave wasn't in sight; there were just some horses grazing peacefully nearby. They looked up as Jeremy approached.

He must be gathering stray cows in the pasture, Jeremy thought. He unlatched the gate and followed the path over the hill. Just then a call came from the barn.

"Jer-e-my!" It sounded urgent!

Jeremy raced back to the barn, rounded the door, and gasped in dismay.

The cows were pushing into the feed bin, mooing,
crowding, and kicking against each other. Oats were spilled
all over the barn floor.

Jeremy had left the feed-bin door open!

Aunt Jeannie's chickens scurried dangerously around the

cows' feet, clucking and pecking at the grain. Calves were crying, and from somewhere Jeremy heard pigs oinking. He stood and stared. It was all his fault.

Uncle Dave gave a shout: "Step back!" He swatted at the cows with his hat.

Ashamed, Jeremy moved aside to let the cows go by. Suddenly from behind came hoofbeats. Confused and scared, Jeremy turned. Uncle Dave's horses were trotting through the open pasture gate—the gate he'd left unlatched! Cows, horses, chickens, and pigs circled in confusion in the barnyard. Jeremy could only huddle against the door next to Barnabas and cry.

Late that afternoon, Jeremy sat sniffling on the stairs next to Aunt Jeannie. What a terrible day! He had turned the barnyard upside down. He had disappointed his uncle. And all this after he had prayed to do a good job!

"Uncle Dave's not mad," Aunt Jeannie said, but that didn't make Jeremy feel any better.

For a long time they sat there, listening to the tick of the grandfather clock. Finally Aunt Jeannie spoke again.

"Remember what I read this morning? God causes all things to work together for good."

Jeremy couldn't imagine any good coming of this day.

That night at dinner, Uncle Dave prayed, thanking God for the day.

How can he? wondered Jeremy, peeking at his uncle. He stared at his plate until the prayer was over. He couldn't understand why Uncle Dave wasn't mad at him . . . or at God. And he didn't understand God, either. Jeremy couldn't think of much to be thankful for.

After dinner, Aunt Jeannie tucked Jeremy into his big, feathery bed. The silky edge of the quilt felt good around his chin. As Aunt Jeannie pulled the drapes closed over the high windows, Jeremy watched Barnabas curl at his feet. He hoped that old Bessie and her friends were okay tonight and the calves had gotten over their fright.

Aunt Jeannie sat on the edge of the bed to pray. "Thank You, dear God, for today . . . for Jeremy being with us . . . for watching over all the animals . . . and for causing everything to work together for good."

Jeremy pouted—he didn't want to pray. Aunt Jeannie just smiled, as if to say she understood, and whispered good-night. Jeremy heard her footsteps on the stairs and listened as she stopped to wind the grandfather clock.

Jeremy squeezed his eyes tightly shut. Tick . . . tock . . . tick . . . tock. He opened his eyes and leaned on his elbow. Yawning, he thought back on the day. Aunt Jeannie said God made things work together for good. *But where was God this morning?*

Tick . . . tock . . . tick . . . tock. *Maybe God doesn't really do much to the world,* Jeremy thought. *Maybe He just winds it up, the way Aunt Jeannie winds the clock, and then goes away and leaves things to run themselves.* The thought worried him.

Tick . . . tock . . . tick . . . tock. The sound made Jeremy sleepy. He pulled the silky edge of his quilt higher. Tick . . . tock. The clock continued to count the minutes.

Suddenly Jeremy sat up. Someone was talking at the foot of his bed. He rubbed his eyes and squinted into the darkness.

"Tsk, tsk. The very idea!"

"Who is it?" Jeremy whispered.

"What a silly idea!" said the voice.

"What's a silly idea?"

"God winding things up like a clock!" It was Barnabas talking!

"Well, isn't that the way God does things?" Jeremy replied, as though talking with cats was something he did every day.

Barnabas arched his back and raised his tail in a question mark. "Jeremy, don't you know? God notices every teensy-weensy detail. How dreadful to suppose that He just . . . just winds things up and walks away! Do you *really* want to know just how much God is in control?" Barnabas swished his orange tail.

"Yes!" Jeremy exclaimed, looking Barnabas straight in the eye. "Yes, I really *do* want to know!"

The big orange cat licked his paw twice, as if thinking, and then began. "As my—ahem—great-great-great-great-great-grandfather passed down the story, there were once upon a time more animals on earth than you could imagine. Far more than on our farm." Barnabas lowered his head, looking over his glasses. "It was at the time of Noah, as you humans have heard.

"Because people did not believe in God," the cat continued, looking knowingly at Jeremy, "God decided to destroy the earth. But first He commanded Noah to build an ark. He told Noah to put two of every living creature on the ark—two of every kind of bird and every kind of animal."

Jeremy cupped his chin in his hands. He'd heard this story before . . . what did it prove?

"Well, just how do you suppose those animals came two by two to Noah's ark?" Barnabas asked. "What if God had simply let things run themselves, as you suggest? Noah would have had one wild barnyard! Imagine him rounding up all those animals by himself! Can't you see him stalking

tigers with traps? Or running after elephants with a net?"

Jeremy clutched his knees and smiled.

"Imagine Noah calling from behind a palm tree: 'Oh, Mr. Hippopotamus, come here . . . and bring your wife.' "

Jeremy giggled.

"Or how in the world," Barnabas continued, "could Noah have caught all those crazy birds? And you know how finicky we cats are. My family would never have stayed in line with two foxes on our tails."

Jeremy laughed aloud.

"And once Noah got them all corralled in the ark, who do you think kept the lions from pouncing on the deer? Or the hyenas from laughing at the wombats because of their silly name? Or the mice from frightening the elephants? Or the dogs from chasing my poor old great-great-great-great-great-grandfather? Don't you think *someone* had to be in control?" Barnabas cocked his head.

Jeremy remembered the confusion in the barnyard today. Noah couldn't have organized such a big bunch of animals alone. Somebody else must have taken charge.

"Well?" the cat asked again.

Jeremy shrugged his shoulders and smiled . . . but inside he knew the answer.

"It was *God* who had control over everything, from mosquitoes to mules. From weasels to wombats. And over my great-great-great-great-great-grandfather and his family, I am relieved to say." Barnabas smiled his funny cat smile.

"But, Barnabas, what about our animals in the barnyard this morning?" Jeremy said. "Where was God then?"

"Why, God still made things work for good," Barnabas answered. He paused, licking a paw. "Didn't *you* learn an important lesson?"

Jeremy lowered his head. "Like being careful instead of trying to impress people?"

Barnabas nodded and smiled a gentle cat smile. . . .

Tick . . . tock . . . tick . . . tock. The sound suddenly seemed loud. Jeremy turned over in bed. There was a footstep in the hallway. Startled, Jeremy jumped up, only to find a purring Barnabas curled in his place near the foot of the bed.

Aunt Jeannie creaked open the bedroom door. "Jeremy, did I hear you call?"

Jeremy looked at Barnabas, who just yawned and continued to sleep.

Aunt Jeannie knelt by his bed and stroked his hair. "Are you still feeling sad, dear?"

At that moment, Uncle Dave walked into the room, knotting the belt on his robe. Jeremy sat up eagerly.

"Barnabas told me . . . I mean, Aunt Jeannie said that God makes things work together for good. I know that now, Uncle Dave," Jeremy said. His uncle sat on the bed beside his aunt. "And I'm really sorry about what happened."

Uncle Dave smiled. Jeremy reached for his uncle's hand and held it tight. Aunt Jeannie hugged them both.

"Why don't we pray together?" she said.

Once again, Jeremy felt all cozy inside. And this time, Jeremy prayed, too.

When everything around you goes haywire, you feel so confused. You might even scratch your head, wondering how God will make it work together for good.

Sometimes, God may simply want to teach you a lesson. Jeremy learned to be careful and not to try to impress his uncle. The Bible talks about that very thing: "Love . . . is neither anxious to impress nor does it cherish inflated ideas of its own importance" (I Corinthians 13:4, Phillips).

Do things seem confused right now around you—at school with your friends or at home with your brother or sister? Don't worry. God is in control. And it may be that He wants to teach you an important lesson, like trusting and obeying Him, or being patient, or being more careful. Whatever the lesson, you can bet it's worth learning—just ask Jeremy!